MW00883211

THE
WORLD
BURNS
A Post-Apocolyptic Story

BOYD CRAVEN

TABLE OF CONTENTS

CHAPTER 1

Blake never had much money, but living frugally was second nature to the guy who did odd jobs for everyone in town and wrote a blog about living off the grid. Most of the work he did was handyman work. None of it was licensed or inspected, but it was good work that would pass. The folks who paid him didn't care about a piece of paper and knew quality when they saw it. Blake loved spending all his free time blogging or outdoors. He spent most of his time in the bottomlands of Kentucky where he lived. Fishing, hunting, and growing a big vegetable garden made for a quiet and solitary lifestyle, and he didn't need much in the way of income.

He'd inherited ten acres from his grandpa that had an old barn full of one hundred years of assorted junk. That was where he built his small homestead. At first he had a camper trailer on site, but as money came in little by little, he started to build a simple home for himself. Being a jack of all trades and master of none, he was easily able to purchase the materials he needed and the equipment necessary to dig and hand-pour a basement. He then spent the next two years building the house. He'd worked as many jobs as he could find, including a paper route, to get all the materials he needed purchased. He finally finished the house of his dreams.

There never was a missus out there; not many ladies would like to live so far away from town, and the only electricity he had was from the twenty-four-volt Uni-Solar roofing he'd bought on the cheap. He used it to power his well and two small chest freezers. One of the freezers was actually converted into a small fridge, and took a lot less energy. He'd found the conversion kit on Amazon of all places for around fifty dollars, made by Johnson Controls. He put those in another portion of the basement where it was cooler, hoping that it would take less energy that way. The Internet was taken care of by a wireless air card and his laptop, or his cell phone. The most expensive part of his house was the big deep-cycle batteries. Blake kept them and the charge controller stored in a special room in the basement so they'd never freeze or get stolen.

The day he moved out of his camper and into the house was a joyous day, and although Blake could have used the propane wall heater in the

THE WORLD BURNS

camper, he instead installed a little potbellied stove for heating and cooking. With two years living through the mild Kentucky winters in a camper, he was more than ready for a little bit of comfort, and he set about finding furniture to fit the house. Wondering where to look first, he was startled by his cell phone breaking the silence.

"Hello? Blake's Handyman Service," he said, not recognizing the number.

"Hi Blake, this is Pastor Duncan. We have a leaky pipe here at the church, and I can't figure things out."

"Ah, hi Pastor. I'll be right over."

"Thanks Blake," he said and hung up the phone. Furniture shopping would have to wait.

Getting into his almost used up 70s Dodge D truck, he prayed the old beast would turn over. The old diesel engine needed some serious work, and he hadn't had the time to do it, as it'd all gone into finishing the house. After a couple tries, the truck belched a dark cloud and rumbled as it idled.

"I should have all the tools already," Blake mumbled to himself.

He headed into town, not knowing how his life was about to change.

CHAPTER 2

O kay Pastor Duncan, I got it all squared away," he told the portly man.

"How much do I owe you?" The pastor had a checkbook out and a pen poised to the paper.

"Well, it's two hours and…" his voice trailed off into nothing as a slender woman came walking in, her dark brown hair cut short, almost in a spike. Most ladies that turned his head had long, flowing hair, but this one was different. She had a presence that made him notice. She had freckles spread across her cheeks and dark green eyes that hinted at the fun and excitement she'd seen in her life.

"Hello, I'm Blake," he held his hand out as she stopped next to the pastor and gave him a quick one-armed hug.

THE WORLD BURNS

"Oh, sorry, how rude of me. Blake, this is my daughter, Sandra. Sandra, this is Blake."

"Pleasure," she said with a smile, showing her teeth. His heart felt like it was laboring to start again, and he couldn't quit staring.

"So Blake…?"

"Huh?" He looked at the priest again.

"How much do I owe you?"

"Well, this is the only church in town and all. How about we call this tithe for this week?"

"Nonsense. What's your usual rate?"

"Thirty-five an hour," he admitted after a pause. "But it was a simple fix. I spent more time showing you how to fix it next time it happens. How about we call it oh…twenty-five dollars, and the rest is tithe?"

"Why twenty-five?" Sandra asked him.

"It's how much a fuel pump costs."

"Is that your truck out front?"

"The one with the tools?" He was glad to have a chance to get the younger lady talking to him. She was an adult, but almost too pretty to look at for long without getting caught staring.

"Yeah, must be. You know how to put one in?"

"A fuel pump? Sort of. I work on just about anything, but it'll be a first with that old beast."

"Here you go," Pastor Duncan smiled as he pushed a check into Blake's breast pocket and left the room unnoticed.

"If you want a hand, I know that truck like the back of my hand."

7

BOYD CRAVEN

"How?" He knew it was dumb to ask, and it probably broke some sort of ethics thing, but a lady, a pretty lady, who knew mechanics?

"Well, the army unit I was stationed with had a ton of them. You get the parts, they run forever. Especially the diesels like you got."

"You were in the army?" Surprise after surprise floored the thirty-year-old man. "You look like you just graduated high school." He winced when he realized how insulting that must have sounded.

"It's okay, you don't have to pull your foot out of your mouth. I get that a lot. I'm actually twenty-eight, and the motor pool was my life until about two months ago."

"Thanks." He laughed in relief at not getting called out for his careless tongue. "Tell you what, I'll be in town again on Friday to pick up an order I have coming in. Maybe we can borrow Pete's Garage, and later on, I'll take you out for something to eat?"

Blake realized not once had he checked out her finger to make sure she was available. He was about to apologize when she smiled and nodded.

"That sounds wonderful actually." She took his hand and gave it a squeeze and wrote her number for him.

He left the church and headed to the bank, surprised when he pulled the check out and found it was made out for one hundred and fifty dollars. He was going to complain, but the money was already being counted by the teller. He could always stuff

THE WORLD BURNS

the rest into the donation basket the next time he was in town for church. It would be awkward to do without an envelope, so he snagged one from the bank and then walked across the street to the supermarket.

"Morning Blake." Sally, his mother's best friend when his family had been alive, greeted him as he walked into the small air-conditioned grocery store. "Picking up supplies?"

"No ma'am, just wanted to get a paper and maybe a bottle or two for later on."

"Oh, no you don't. I'll swat you down if you try to buy some—"

Sally broke into a smile as Blake got two Diet Cokes from the refrigerated case and put them on the counter along with a newspaper. If he was in town, he might as well check Craigslist ads and the paper before heading back home. Trips to town cost him in terms of fuel, and though he lived a frugal life by necessity, he had brought some cash of his own just in case he found something.

"That'll be four dollars and five cents, hon." She smiled. He paid her and left the store.

The heat in the truck hit him like a ton of bricks, but Blake rolled down the windows and spread out the newspaper before cracking into his first cola. The advertisement page held almost nothing of interest. At least, nothing that wasn't way too expensive. He was about to give up and check Craigslist on his phone when he saw an advertisement that caught his eye. *Storage Unit Auctions, Friday July*

BOYD CRAVEN

9th, 2 p.m. Smiling, he started the truck and headed back towards the house, the thirty minute drive soothing despite the deep ruts of the two-track lane.

CHAPTER 3

Blake didn't get any more calls that week for folks needing a handyman, so he used some of the camping furniture in the house. He had fun testing out the gray water system he had set up on his sink and shower. Just having a pressurized shower felt luxurious. He'd easily made his water heater using one-inch pex tubing and coiling it inside an insulated box covered in glass. The whole thing was mounted on the roof. With only one side dedicated to solar, the other was still available. The pipes ran down to the basement and fed throughout the house wherever hot water was needed.

Friday came after a long week of gardening, and he spent a little more time on how he looked. He trimmed his hair the best he could and had the best shave ever, now that he had a big mirror to stand in front of in his otherwise empty house. If he planned things out right, he could get the parts, go fix the truck, go to the auction, and then go on a date. It'd been years since he'd last gone on one, and Blake stressed over what to wear. In the end, he put on his best shirt and the best jeans he had with a clean pair of work boots. He hitched up an enclosed trailer he'd had forever to his truck so he had extra room to haul his findings

After leaving the auto parts store, he thumbed in Sandra's number and waited for her to pick up.

"Hello?" Her voice was music to him.

"Hi, this is Blake. I'm in town today doing some stuff and—"

"Great! I already talked to Pete, and he said we can use the bay with the lift."

"You know Pete?"

"Of course. I went to school with his daughter. I've been working off and on for a day or two there to have some rolling around money."

He laughed. "That's good news. When do you want to—"

"I'm ready now if you are. Meet you there."

"Okay, I'll see you soon." He hung up.

He pulled into Pete's parking lot and dropped the trailer in one of the back parking spots. He noticed Sandra immediately. He pulled in as she directed him and stopped. For an hour they worked on the truck, and Blake learned a ton of new tricks on diesel maintenance. With a new fuel pump and

THE WORLD BURNS

water filter, some tweaks and vacuum tubes replaced, the truck was purring like a kitten.

"What's the Trailer for?" Sandra asked him as they were washing their hands with some goop.

"Well, I just finished building my house, but I've been sleeping on the floor…So…I thought I'd go to an auction today and see if they had any beds, chairs. That sort of thing."

"Sleeping on the floor? Why would you do that?"

"It's better than the camper, trust me." He smiled at the bemused look she gave him.

"You can't live in a camper in town. Where are you?"

"Out on Holloway Trail."

"That isn't a trail, that's an old logging track."

"I have ten acres up there I got from my grandparents. Nice and quiet."

"I bet. Well, let's go to the auction then."

"Uh, I didn't ask you because, I mean, you're welcome to come of course but," he stammered.

"You didn't think I'd want to go to something so boring? No, I won't consider that part a date… and you have to quit thinking you'll stick your foot in your mouth around me. I'm just a normal girl."

He took a few deep breaths. "Sounds good to me."

They hitched the trailer back on the truck and took off to the storage unit almost thirty minutes before the auction started.

"You ever been to one of these?" Sandra asked.

13

"No, but I brought some cash in case I find something."

"It looks pretty dead here."

Sandra was right. Other than one car, the parking lot to the storage units was empty. They got out of the truck and headed into the office area where an elderly lady looked up hopefully from a newspaper.

"Here for the auction, dears?"

"Yes, ma'am."

"Well, it isn't a big one. I've got two units today. We'll wait until two and then head out there. Does that sound okay to you?"

"I'm fine with that. We're early," he explained.

"Better too early than late, I always say," she cackled.

The woman introduced herself as Ethel, and Blake and Sandra gave her their names and shook her hand. The ladies talked and Blake only half listened as he looked at the newspaper she had been reading. There was news that the nuclear talks with Iran were not going well, and a new round of terrorism was sweeping across Europe. He doubted anything like that would ever touch him in America's heartland, but it was something he hadn't been paying attention to in the past week. Not since he'd met the pastor's daughter that is.

When it was 2 p.m., the three of them walked out alone. Ethel held out a pair of bolt cutters to Blake.

"You do the honors."

THE WORLD BURNS

"Okay," he told her. He broke the lock open and rolled up the door.

The storage unit had a mattress on the left wall, and floor to ceiling boxes as far as he could see. Blake started to move one before his hand was slapped.

"No, gotta bid on them without knowing. Haven't you seen the TV show?"

"How do I know if I want it?"

"It's a gamble."

"Well, where's the other one?" he asked.

"Right there." She pointed out a door across from the one that had been cracked open.

Blake cut the lock on that one and smiled when the door rolled up. There was a dining set with matching chairs stored upside down around a table for four. A Lazy Boy recliner and a desk were pushed against one wall, and some boxes and trash bags full of what he would guess to be clothing made up the rest of the unit. It wasn't full, but it looked promising to him, though it didn't have a bed.

"So how much for this one?"

"You bid."

"What happens if nobody bids on anything?" he asked her.

"I keep it and throw away what I don't want… but by law I have to offer it up for bid first."

"Twenty dollars," he started. She laughed.

"You're cheap, boy."

"Well, I had to start somewhere."

BOYD CRAVEN

"There isn't anyone else here to bid. Tell you what, eighty dollars a unit if you take both."

"I don't know if I want that other one, but it does have a mattress…"

"Or it's one-fifty for the one with the table and chairs."

Blake cursed himself for a fool and smiled. This woman didn't want to dig through the units to sort out the treasure, she just wanted both of them gone. He pulled out his wallet and peeled out eight bills and handed them to her. She thanked him and went inside to get a receipt.

"So, was that like TV?" Blake asked Sandra, who surprised him by laughing out loud, covering her mouth as the funny worked itself out.

"No, that was nothing like *Storage Wars*. You just got taken advantage of by a little old lady."

"Well shucks, not really. That table and chairs is worth that alone. I am just frugal by nature," he admitted.

"Or cheap."

"You picking on me there, Ms. Preacher's daughter?"

"Yes, yes I am."

Before he could stick his foot in his mouth more, he walked back to his pickup truck, tongue-tied. He pulled the truck down the middle lane between both units. Ethel came back out with a sheet of paper.

"All right, here's your receipt. You two get these unloaded in the next few hours, or the rest is going

THE WORLD BURNS

into the dumpster."

"I can manage that," Blake told her and she nodded.

"You two newlyweds have fun, I've got soaps to watch." She walked off, her shoulders straight and proud.

Blake opened his mouth to speak, but all his air left him in a rush when a hand poked him in the side and surprised the crap out of him.

"Come on hubs, let's get loading," she joked.

"Which one should we do first?"

"How about the mattress and boxes against the back wall of the trailer, then we can throw the rest of the stuff in the bed of the truck if we run out of room."

"That's what I was thinking."

They both started to load boxes into the trailer, but Blake was worried that if the entire unit was full of boxes, he'd run out of room. That wasn't the case. There was only a two-layer set of boxes deep and high. Most of the unit was actually hollowed out, but what he saw had him instantly stunned. There was an old three-wheeler and a quad parked by the back wall, and a black metal safe still strapped to a dolly with solid rubber wheels.

"Jackpot," he mumbled.

Something in his voice made Sandra look back, and her jaw dropped open.

"Do you think they run?" he asked her, running his hands over the old Hondas.

"If they don't, I can fix them easily." She was

17

smiling.

"Of course you can."

"Let's get these loaded before the old lady comes out and decides to charge you more."

They both worked in a hurry, putting the Hondas into the front of the trailer and then loading boxes on and behind them, making a solid blocking wall. The mattress went next, and they found a small metal frame when they rolled the safe in. The safe wasn't as heavy as they expected it to be, but it had something inside that shifted and banged when it was moved. Sandra guessed it held guns. It was the right size, but there were no markings, and even worse, no keys.

The last unit, the one that Blake wanted the most, was also the easiest to load. That one took little time, and as they were rolling down the doors, Ethel came out to wish them luck and to see if they had left a mess for her. When she saw they hadn't, she smiled and wished them a happy life together. Blake made it until they were in the truck and almost pulling out until he busted up laughing.

"What's so funny?"

"You smiled when she said that, like you think—" then he stopped dead. "I almost did it again, didn't I?" he asked her.

"You don't get out much, do you?"

"You have no idea! So where would you like to grab a bite to eat today?"

"Well, let's get this stuff unloaded at your place, and then we'll figure something out."

THE WORLD BURNS

Blake just nodded. He hadn't intended on going back so early, but now that he had her in the truck with him, he didn't want to spend any time apart. Finding a lady who caught his interest was hard enough, finding a lady who could put up with his foot in mouth disease was almost impossible when you added the two things together. He drove the loaded down truck out of town slowly.

"Do you think you're dad will get the wrong idea about you helping me unload things?"

"What, that a single woman who's an adult with military training cannot handle herself in a proper manner around a roughened hermit who may or may not be an axe murderer?"

"I wouldn't use an axe. I have a chainsaw." He busted up laughing when her jaw dropped open.

"See, you are starting to loosen up around me. Joking—jokes are good, Mister Funny Man."

"Thanks. I don't know, you don't scare me so much now."

"Scare you?"

"Well, you know." His face was burning.

"Scare you?" she pressed.

"You're pretty, but you are Pastor Duncan's daughter, and I don't want to screw this up. It scares me."

"My my, love at first sight?" she asked, watching him turn a shade of crimson.

"I'm about to die of a stroke. Let me pull off the lane so I can die without taking you with me first."

"Okay, okay, I won't pick on you. Thank you

though."

"For what?"

"For calling me pretty. Most guys won't give me a second look. I know you don't mean it—nobody likes a greasy tomboy hanging around. I'm just glad you took pity on me. It's lonely sometimes."

"You're joking right?" Blake asked, not understanding her tone of voice. She didn't sound like she had earlier when she was joking.

She never answered, and he didn't press. His turn off for Holloway Trail was coming, and it took all his concentration to get the trailer straight on the path because the turns didn't leave much room with the trees closing in on both sides. Sandra had been right; this lane was little more than an old logging trail. It had a full canopy of trees across it, the branches sometimes brushing noisily across the top of the trailer. They came to a spot, and Blake drove the truck slowly through and stopped, jumping out.

"What are you doing?" Sandra yelled.

"Making sure I don't rip the jack off the trailer. It's loaded down more than I'd normally like. The ruts in the road are bad here."

After a moment of inspection, they started rolling slowly. Even raised and turned sideways, it rubbed on the ground, but it didn't cause any issues. After that spot, the drive got easier until the lane ended.

"Where's your house?" Sandra asked as he turned left into an old cow pasture and skirted the fence line.

THE WORLD BURNS

"Up and over the hill."

"It's way back there?"

"Yeah."

"How do you get out in the winter time?"

"Uh, I don't."

"You mean, you live up here alone, all winter?"

"Yeah."

"I take that back, you weren't joking about the chainsaw, were you?"

"Nope." He grinned and concentrated on the drive.

Another ten minutes of bone-jarring bumps and he was pulling in front of his small house. Almost self-consciously, he wished he would have parked his old camper trailer out back. He'd lived there alone for years by himself, and he'd never had to worry about what a lady would think. In fact, she was the first person to come back here since he'd started construction. Blake decided he needed to get out more. Maybe he was living his life too much on his blogs and by himself.

"Wow, this place is so cool...Oh shit," Sandra said and then covered her mouth.

"What?" Blake asked, worried the place looked too unkempt. Truth was, he never mowed around the house unless the grass got more than waist high. He only used the old diesel tractor once a year to cut paths through the property where he wanted to go.

"That trailer."

Blake groaned inwardly.

BOYD CRAVEN

"It's like the one in this blog I've been reading… Oh my God, you're Back Country J?"

Blake was worse than speechless; he was tongue-tied yet again. He knew his blog got readers, because folks used the affiliate links he put up, and he got the occasional comment on his writing. Mostly a request for more pictures or to explain something better, but he'd never run into or talked to somebody who'd read it. Not face to face.

"Oh, this is great! You must show me around!" She was bossy in such a way that he had to comply. He killed his engine and followed her as she bypassed the house and ran through the grass towards the camper.

"This, how many nights did you sit inside here with that little solar panel you talked about? Writing?"

"Almost every night," he admitted.

"Oh, and the house. You finished? You hadn't said on your blog. Latest update was the French drains you put in around your fruit—oh my gosh, there they are."

Blake let her walk around and tell him all about his homestead. It was somewhat embarrassing how much she knew about him, and she hadn't realized it was him the entire time. He figured everybody knew about the hermit of Holloway Trail, but he'd never posted a picture of himself. She stopped at the barn and raised an eyebrow.

"You never took pictures of inside the barn, just the outside. How come?"

THE WORLD BURNS

"It's full of old junk, scrap, glass and such. Never cleaned it out, and I guess I was too frugal to pay to have a scrapper come out and clean it up."

"Cheap."

"Frugal," he said, but he was smiling as she darted inside.

There were no lights in the barn, but sunlight filtered through the slats of wood. This hadn't been an insulated barn meant for keeping animals, but one that would hold a lot of hay, a tractor, or other equipment. When he showed her the stairs leading down to the root cellar, Sandra made a sound that he'd never heard, but had read about. He believed she actually "squeed." Whatever that meant, it was a happy sound.

"Why no lights?"

"Too much voltage drop from the battery banks," he admitted, the house being quite a distance from the barn.

"Wait, you have lights. Kerosene lanterns." She pointed to the wall.

"Well, yeah, but I thought you meant just electric stuff."

"Can we light one and go down?"

"It's just a hole in the ground where I store things."

"I know what a root cellar is, I've just never seen one. You blogged about yours, but I never could figure out where it was."

"Well, to be honest, it's a dirty hole in the ground with earth floors. I didn't want to take pictures of it."

"Please?"

"Okay." He grabbed a box of matches on a work bench and got a lantern lit. They walked down the block cement stairs until they stopped at a heavy wooden door on the bottom.

"This has been here long before my grandparents. I think this is the root cellar from the original farm, but I'm not for sure."

He pushed the door open and held the lantern up high.

"Oh wow. Like, wow. *Doomsday Preppers* would have a fit if they ever saw this."

"What do you mean?"

Blake was confused. She was walking down the twenty-foot row of shelves that lined either side of the cellar, pausing to look into the bins. The potatoes and carrots were labeled and on the bottom stacks, the carrots packed in loose mason sand that was damp. The potatoes were in bins that let the air in, and higher up on the shelves were crates of apples. Actually, the apples were almost on top of every shelf, with an old wooden crate of pears placed here and there.

"This isn't the only modification that's been done to it in the last hundred years." He pointed to a metal piece of ductwork that came down from the ceiling.

Sandra got underneath of it, frowning, and then put her hand up to it, feeling the draft.

"I didn't think you had power out here?"

THE WORLD BURNS

"It's a little solar setup with a DC duct fan. It wasn't much to rig up. Keeps the air fresh and the ethylene from the apples from ripening everything until it's overdone."

"How does the air flow in?"

"Right now, through the cracks under the door."

"Wow. How do you keep the critters out of here?"

"Well, two ways. I have a screen over the vent up on the main floor, and there's a whole passel of barn cats that people always donate out here."

"You still have Mr. Fluffy Buttons?" she asked, referring to a cat on his blog that almost made grumpy cat green with envy.

"No," he said sadly. "An owl got him about two months ago. I had to put him down after he fought his way free."

"This is so cool. Back Country J. Wait until I tell my dad." She was all smiles, but Blake had a serious look on his face.

"Please don't. I just like things quiet around here."

"Daddy's a fan of your blog. He's the one who told the preppers in the area about it."

"Preppers? Your dad?"

"Yeah. You don't really talk about prepping, but most of the stuff you talk about goes hand in hand with prepping."

"I always thought putting some extra back was good common sense. Like money in the bank."

"Oh God, I'm dying to ask. This place, it cost

BOYD CRAVEN

like millions to set up, didn't it?"

"No, not really. I mean, I'm just a handyman. I'd buy a board when I could afford one, I'd recycle materials from old jobs when I had a chance, and I built things out here."

"No wonder you always used hand tools in your blog. You didn't have electricity…"

"Well, it was an off-grid blog…"

"I never thought you were truly off-grid, but wow."

"Okay, can we go upstairs? This is kind of embarrassing me."

"Okay, okay. But wow. We will so have to talk about this again sometime."

"We can, I'm just not used to people. You're the first one up here since I started on the house."

Sandra's jaw dropped open, and she stepped close to Blake and gave him a hug, then left the cellar, leaving him flustered and confused.

"Thank you," he told the empty room before blowing out the lamp and closing the door.

CHAPTER 4

It took them two hours to unload the trailer, most of it going into the barn for now. The safe was rolled into the house, and Sandra promptly walked out of the house towards the barn. She came back moments later with a cold chisel and a two-pound sledge from the work bench in the barn.

"You don't mind, do you?" she asked, looking at the tools in her hands.

"No, no. Go ahead. It's not like I live here or anything."

"Humor, good. It's starting to come back. Seriously though, you want the honors?"

"No, go ahead. I've never cracked a safe before."

"If it's anything like a vending machine…" She pushed the chisel against a seam in the metal and swung with all her might.

BOYD CRAVEN

Blake was surprised when the metal was forced apart, bending as it went. She changed the angle of the chisel and hit it half a dozen times more and finally wedged the door open.

"Sheet metal, and it's not too thick," she explained before opening the big door all the way.

I wasn't surprised to see the gun inside, but I was surprised to see a note taped inside the back of the safe in a Ziploc bag. Sandra was reaching for the rifle when I started to read the note out loud.

> *Ben, your pistols are in one of the blue totes wrapped in oilcloth. Didn't want you to come back here and freak out when dad's rifle was the only thing in the safe. That way you can grab and go. The keys to the quads and cabin are in there too. Safe was too heavy to move by myself with everything in it.*
>
> *Love ya bro,*
> *Corey*

"I think we better go through those boxes soon," Blake told her.

"What's this we thing? I'm hungry. What's for dinner, Mr. Back Country?"

"Well, what do you like? There's Clyde's Diner, or, if you want a drive, we could catch dinner and a movie at that new place in—"

"I'll have whatever you're cooking." Her smile was sweet, but Blake wasn't used to having a woman around him that made him jump to her every command. Willingly even.

"Well, I have some venison steaks I took out to thaw in the fridge. I could grill some of those up with some baked potatoes and such," he said after a pause.

"That sounds great. Is there a fire pit some-where I can light for you, or do you need me to go pull stuff out of the garden or…"

"I have a gas grill out on the back porch, or we can use the griddle here inside."

"Sorry, I just got a little carried away."

"Just because I show how to do that stuff doesn't mean I always do it like that. I do have some mod-ern conveniences."

"Fair enough. What can I do?"

"Park it right there and I'll be right back."

Blake got the ingredients out from the freezer chest fridge and carried them upstairs. He washed two potatoes and wrapped them in foil and threw them over the flames on one side of a propane burner. It wasn't an oven, but it worked just like grilling your baked potatoes. Then he set up an old cast iron griddle on the other side and turned on the heat, making sure the ribbed surface was good and hot before unwrapping two thick steaks and throwing them on to cook.

"I'll be right back." He disappeared back into the basement and came back up with a green bottle and a cork that'd seen better days.

"What's that?"

"A little fruit wine. I didn't expect company, so I

have wine, water or—"

"Wine is great!" They were both smiling, starting to relax around each other.

Dinner was a big hit, and they went out on the porch to sit on the steps side by side. There was only an hour of full daylight left, and without his phone on him, he could only guess at the time. They sat in companionable silence for a while. When she stood, he followed suit, not knowing what to say or what to do. They'd talked for a long time, and there was so much more he wanted to hear about her, but the day was almost over, and he'd have to drive her home soon or risk the drive in the darkness by himself.

"That was great. I really had a lot of fun." She looked at him awkwardly, and he wondered if she was thinking about a first kiss.

It was plain to both of them that they liked each other, but neither of them had voiced it. The moment stretched, neither of them sure. Blake didn't want her to think he was too forward, and Sandra seemed reluctant to make the lonely man uncomfortable. She'd done that plenty of times just by being excited and interested in everything. In the end, she wrapped her arms around him and hugged him. They stayed like that a long moment, and she took his hand, pulling him off the porch towards the truck.

"I told Dad I'd be home before dark."

"Oh God, I almost hate to ask, what did your dad think of, uh…"

THE WORLD BURNS

"The date?"

"Yeah."

"He told me, 'Good, it's about time somebody got you out of the hills.'"

"Well, at the end of the day, I'm still up here."

"Yes, you are. Let's go."

Beneath them, the ground started to shake. She squeezed his hand, and they were thrown off their feet. The noise was so loud; they couldn't describe it if they had the words to, but the closest any of them would later admit was it sounded like a freight train going off the tracks.

"Earthquake?" Blake asked, not believing it himself.

"Owwwww." Sandra was holding her head. Once the ground quit shaking, she stood.

"Are you okay?"

"I hit my head on your big foot when I fell. I'm fine."

Blake brushed the debris out of her short hair and then dusted his pants off.

"I wonder what that was?" she said.

"I don't know, but look at that," Blake told her, pointing to the rising cloud of smoke.

"Oh God, the town. Hurry." Her voice was frantic as she rounded the truck and slid in.

Blake got the truck fired up and tore off down the lane.

"My battery is dead on my phone," she said after a few moments of pushing buttons and cursing the device.

"Here, use mine." Blake pulled his phone out of his pocket and handed it to her, trying to concentrate on the two-track so he didn't wreck the truck. He'd never tried to travel this stretch this fast.

"Yours is dead too."

"It can't be. It was on the charger during dinner," he muttered, taking his eyes off the road a second to look at it.

"Look out!" She threw her hands up to protect her face and Blake slammed on the breaks, skidding forward.

They were truly blessed that Blake missed the stump. He took a couple of deep breaths to clear his head before reversing the truck and putting it back on the path he'd almost left.

"The radio isn't working," he muttered after fiddling with it.

"Oh shit, I hope I'm wrong."

"What?"

"Blake, something bad has happened. I hope I'm wrong."

"What?"

"Let's get to town."

"No, what? What do you think?"

"Your truck is running, right?"

"Yeah." He was a little confused by her question.

"But you have a newer radio, and both of our phones are dead."

"So, what's that mean?"

"Blake, this is tinfoil hat time, OK? You with me, Blake?"

THE WORLD BURNS

"Okay, sure."

"In the army, there was a study done on the effect of EMPs."

"I know what an EMP is; you think we got hit with one?"

"I don't know. I don't have enough information yet, but…"

Blake had finally driven to the end of the lane and to the edge of the divided highway where the trees parted to show the roadway. There weren't any cars nearby, but off in the distance, they could see people stopped and walking in the road.

"Oh God, this isn't good. We have to check on my father."

"We will," he downshifted and took off, weaving through the stalled traffic when he came to it. People were standing by their dead cars.

For a moment, they both looked at each other. Then they felt the earth shaking. Blake slammed on the breaks as a large cloud of smoke mushroomed up a mile ahead of them. Flames flickered at the edges of Blake's vision, and a wave of heat hit them.

"We have to turn around."

"It's the wrong way," Blake said, not thinking.

"Do it, hurry!"

His driving instructor from years ago wouldn't have approved of the turn he made, and soon they both were sweating as the heat continued to build within the cab. The fires had started to consume everything on the south side of the highway, with the median starting to smolder. Blake swore softly under his breath and pushed the pedal down harder, the stranded cars and people becoming blurs. He slowed finally when they reached Holloway Lane. They were almost going as fast as they came down it, the suspension groaning as the truck bounced all over the track.

"Do you think the fire will reach all the way up here?"

"I don't know. It was moving awfully fast. I don't know what set it off, but I bet you it's from what we felt when the ground shook."

"It felt like a big bomb went off."

"You know, if we go to the back of my property, on top of the hill, there's an old grain silo. When I was a kid, I could see the entire valley from up there."

"I'm worried about my dad," Sandra admitted.

"I know. Right now, we have to make sure we're safe and the fire hasn't spread."

"What if it has?"

"I wait for the wind to shift and start a backfire. I'm hoping the wide median across the highway will work as a firebreak. I've never set one before."

"Me neither. I was mainly a door gunner and mechanic," her voice was coming out strained from the tension.

After long minutes, they made it to the top of the hill, but Blake didn't stop. He kept driving past the barn, leaving the mowed path. He stayed about ten feet away from the fence line, his pickup slipping in the tall grass as the pitch of the hill increased. Finally, he stopped next to an old stone structure, the roof fallen in long ago.

"Hurry," Sandra's voice was cracked with worry.

They both scurried up the rusty steel rungs until they reached the top. Sandra was transfixed with the hollow yawning hole of the silo, the perfect blackness below the edge. Blake was sitting with one leg over each side of the edge of the silo, his mouth gaping wide open.

"Sandra, look." His voice was almost a moan.

What she saw shocked her. There were two clear lines of destruction to the city below, and fire spreading from there on out.

"Oh dear God," she murmured. "That looks like a crashed jet."

"God no, that can't be right."

"That looks like the same line of wreckage that happened in the Pentagon on 9/11. It was something we had to study in our emergency response training. Oh God, Dad, the church," she sobbed.

Blake took in her tearstained cheeks and wanted to hold her, to comfort her, but the weight of his realization had him dumbfounded. He watched the fire march up to the highway, consuming everything in its path. They were too far away to make out cars or people, but he prayed that all living folks had fled. His breath caught when part of the median caught fire, but its path stopped as it hit the water of the drainage running down the center. They sat like that for hours, waiting and watching until the air became unbearable. The smoke was getting too thick, so they made their way to the ground, which was only slightly better.

"Do you think my dad is okay?"

"I hope so," he told her truthfully.

They crawled down slowly and got in the truck, driving the rest of the way to the house. Both of them were too exhausted, and Blake asked if Sandra wanted the mattress or the bedroom or the living room. She sat down on the floor next to where Blake was standing. Confused, he sat down next to her and she wrapped her arms around him, squeezing. They fell into an exhausted sleep like that, and awoke in the morning with stiff and sore muscles.

CHAPTER 5

They both stretched and used the restroom. Blake went throughout the house checking on things, and to his surprise, all the electrical stuff in the house except for his cell phone and laptop, which had been upstairs, didn't work. Sandra noticed that right away and raised an eyebrow before asking, "How is it the lights are working?"

"Let's go check the basement."

They headed down, and he showed her his room he kept the batteries and charge controller in, how it was insulated with foil-backed material to ward off the damp and moisture.

"Wow, it must have shielded everything down here. Your well is underground too, isn't it?"

"Yeah. It was a pain but—"

"Do you think we can go outside and look?"

"We probably should."

They headed outside where the smell of smoke was more noticeable. Neither of them could see any fire coming up towards Blake's house. They both looked at the truck, then looked at each other.

"Maybe we should drive down and check," Blake said after a moment.

"Sure," Sandra told him, but he could tell that her soul was heavy with worry.

The old truck started up and ran as well as it had the day before, and soon they were at the end of the lane. Blake shut off the engine and hopped out. The fire had consumed everything across the divided highway, and parts of the tall grass in the median had burned all the way down to the soil. Ash covered everything like white powdery snow, and when the wind picked up, the heat was still almost unbearable.

"It looks like it's out over here." He looked to see if Sandra had heard him.

"Do you think it's safe? To go into town?"

"We can try."

Both of them were scared of what they'd find, but with the worst of the danger gone, information and finding Pastor Duncan became their top priority. They drove for about five minutes when it became obvious that they couldn't go any further. Waves of heat washed over them as they drove closer to the site of impact, and when the wind blew, ashes would swirl, obscuring the views. Thick col-

THE WORLD BURNS

umns of smoke rose into the distance, and it looked as if the gates of hell had opened, consuming everything in its path.

"I don't think I can keep going. The fires are still burning, and its—" He stopped when a loud sob interrupted him.

"My dad. I hope…Blake, my dad was going to head to the late show to see the new Terminator movie. Do you know what time everything went out?"

"It felt like we had an hour of daylight left. I'm guessing maybe eight p.m.?" He felt bad when she cried harder.

"What's wrong?"

"His movie got done at six thirty. He teased me about being a good girl and me beating him home. It's why I didn't think of mentioning it yesterday."

Blake got the truck turned around about half a mile closer to town than he had made it yesterday and spoke softly. "Did he head into Greenville for the movies, or did he go to the little one-screen place by the old mall?"

"Greenville, why?"

"Traffic. On a smooth day it's about an hour from town to Greenville."

"So he might be out there?"

"Yeah, it's possible."

"I can't think like this." She took long, deep breaths and closed her eyes a moment.

When she opened her eyes, her personality shifted slightly, and a calmer Sandra looked over at

Blake.

"Can we drive towards Greenville?"

"Yeah, but do you think we can get past all the stalled cars? This isn't too bad here, but it's probably a nightmare further up the road."

"Only one way to check."

They were silent as they drove past the turn off for Blake's homestead and headed towards Greenville. The fire hadn't come as close to the highway here as it had where they assumed the jet crashed back towards the smaller town. The cars started to get thicker and thicker, and they saw people raising their heads above the seats as they slowly rumbled past. Some got out to stand in the road, and many of them shouted questions, begging for information and rides. Blake slowed down when he saw a mother and her two daughters waving him down. He had to stop or hit her. Her black sedan was gray with falling ash.

"How is it your truck is running? Do you know what's going on here?"

"No, not really. My truck is old, so it doesn't have electronics in the motor. I think that's what makes the difference."

"Hey mister, can you give me a ride into Greenville?" The voice was masculine, and he turned to see about ten folks who'd slept in their cars approaching him slowly.

"Hey, why is your truck working and ours aren't?" another voice shouted.

Blake didn't panic, but he knew he was getting

THE WORLD BURNS

boxed in, and they needed to move.

"Ma'am, you and your daughters okay here? Do you need anything?"

"No, we slept in the car fine. I'm sure the wreckers will be coming to help us soon."

"Please don't count on that. You three could come with us."

"What about us?" another voice shouted.

"No, we'll be fine here." She smiled at him, trusting the government to put the genie back into the bottle.

"Okay." Blake turned and walked past some of the folks who were starting to surround him. He saw Sandra lean over and unlock his door as he got close, and he began to open it when somebody grabbed him by the arm and spun him around.

"Hey, I asked you a question. Can you give me a ride to Greenville?" The irate man from earlier was red in the face.

"No. No, I can't," he shrugged off the hand.

A sudden shifting in the belligerent man's eyes alerted Blake, and he was able to move his head quick enough to only get a glancing blow to the side of his face by the thrown punch. The stranger's fist hit the solid side behind the door panel and left a small dent. He howled and shook his hand. Blake shoved him roughly back and jumped in the truck, locking the door.

"You have to get us out of here quick, or we're going to have to run some over."

"If they don't move, I will," Blake growled, feeling his ear with his left hand as he shifted the truck into reverse.

People blocked his path, but they started moving when he slowly bumped into the man closest to his truck. The man's friends had to pull him out of the way as Blake continued to back out of traffic. Hands slapped at the bed of the truck and the hood, but he ignored the angry protests until he found a large open spot and turned the truck around before speeding off.

"Wow, that almost got really ugly. I'm not leaving the house without my gun next time," Blake said.

"You would have been safe."

"You have a gun in that little clutch?" He realized by the expression she gave him that he'd done it again.

"No…" She pulled a small Beretta from her back waistband and set it on her lap.

"You any good with that?"

"Just because I was mainly in the motor pool doesn't mean I don't know how to use one of these things. Let's just go back to your place. I'm sorry I almost got you hurt out there."

"Why are you sorry?"

"Because I think you're right. Dad's car is in that traffic back there somewhere. He has to be. I just panicked, and now that reality is kicking in…"

"Please don't tell me it's not as bad as I think?" Blake asked her.

"No, Dad's former military, just like me. He's

also a hardcore prepper. He'll have his bag in his car."

"Bug-out bag?" Blake asked, familiar with a lot of the terminology that preppers used. It was also common in the homesteading movement.

"Yeah. I just pray he was stuck outside of town when that blast went off. The way the fire was blazing, it looked like the whole world was burning."

"Yeah, it looked pretty bad. I know the fires aren't out, but I can't make them out in the distance in this daylight. So if this is an EMP, what should we be doing? I mean, almost everything back at my place was saved somehow."

"It's how you did that room in the basement I think."

"What do you mean?"

They turned down his lane, and he had to concentrate on the road or otherwise lose his truck to the ruts again.

"Well, you have your electrical stuff grounded to your well. The room is basically a big grounded metal box underground."

"It's not metal."

"How many layers of that foil-backed insulation do you have?"

"Three or four," he admitted. "It was all I had leftover from a couple of jobs. I was going to use something else, but it's what I had at the time."

"Okay, let's just hurry. I told my dad you lived on Holloway Lane. Maybe he's going to make his way here if he's alive." A single tear escaped her eye, and she looked away into the underbrush.

They drove in silence until he killed the motor, parking between the house and the barn.

"What should we do?" Blake asked her again.

"How are you set for food?"

"You saw my garden. That's about it, unless we go do some hunting. I never got a chance to pick up my supplies from town."

"Without those, do you think we have enough food for two weeks or more?"

"Two weeks? Sure. Easily."

"I'm going to be peeling a lot of potatoes, aren't I?" She smiled a moment, looking at him.

"We both are."

"Let's get some food, and we'll take some sort of inventory."

"You sure are bossy," Blake teased. She took it in stride.

"All part of the job."

CHAPTER 6

The next week was spent in the garden and in the barn. Sandra insisted on going through everything to inventory it. She tried to hide her annoyance when she'd ask how much of something Blake had. He'd always point and say "a lot" or "running low." Right away, Sandra became the list maker and organizer as they finished unpacking the furniture into the house. Their evenings ended early with the daylight, and they took turns on the bed or the recliner. Every box that they had unloaded into the barn was gone through with a fine-tooth comb, and the storage unit that Blake was going to pass on, except for the mattress, contained almost a full wardrobe of lady's clothing.

The rest of the guns were located, along with a Ziploc bag full of documents, including the rental agreement to the storage unit. They poured through it and found out that the owner, Corey, was a lady who'd moved into an apartment in town, according to the address. She probably never had room to store the quads and safe, so she rented a unit. Blake wondered aloud what might have happened to her, but Sandra just shook her head.

One other find that excited her was a box full of books. Four of them were from the Foxfire series, and she did a happy dance until Blake made her calm down and explain to him what that meant. They would have tried to drive to town, but they were too worried that another ugly incident would happen.

When it became apparent to Blake that she was hell-bent on sorting through everything, he left her to it so he didn't have to slow her down. He had thoughts of venison, and although it was out of season, he couldn't just go to the grocery store anymore, so he went into the camper trailer and got out his long gun and a small box of ammunition, his backpack and knife, then set out for the field on foot.

"Is everything okay?" Sandra asked, seeing him in his camo shirt and hat, armed for the first time with his rifle.

"I'm going to go get some venison for the freezer."

"Okay, I'll be right here—"

"Sorting through everything."

They laughed and let it go. They'd only lived under one roof for a little under a week, but already they understood that sometimes people need a little space. Blake could tell Sandra had been trying not to get under his skin with her excitement and obsessive list making, and he knew it drove her crazy that he lived every prepper's dream lifestyle and he was so blasé about it. He had no clue how many pounds of produce he had in the root cellar, and when he needed meat, he would do what he was doing right now, go hunting. He had little in the way of material possessions, but he lived a simpler life. Somehow he got the feeling that Sandra appreciated that kind of life, and he was growing more and more sure that she wanted to be a part of it.

§ § §

Blake was still out hunting when dark fell. Not long after he fired a single shot, Sandra came running toward him. She was calling out to him, panic in her voice. And not only that, she had her Beretta raised and aimed in one hand, and a sandwich in the other. She looked as though she had been right in the middle of making dinner when she'd heard his gun go off. The panic left her eyes when she saw it was him, and he smiled. "Hey, great, you brought me dinner." Blake smiled wider as he walked up to her and took the sandwich from her shaking hand.

"Dammit, Blake. You didn't tell me you were going to be gone all day and half the night."

"I didn't know I was going to either. I didn't see

any deer, but I did run across some running bacon."

"Bacon?"

"Look," he pointed to the gloom.

She approached it, irked that he'd assumed the sandwich was his, but she smiled when she almost tripped over a black-furred shaggy creature.

"They sure smell in real life."

"Yeah. I jumped this hog heading in for dinner."

"I'm surprised you could see him in the dark. It looks like a spine shot."

"Yeah, I had to wait for him to step into some good lighting, otherwise I was going to drag you out here tomorrow and help me find their sounder."

"Sounder?"

"Group of pigs. Family unit."

"Oh. Uh…that thing is bigger than you. How are we going to get it back?"

"Did you ever get a chance to check those quads out?" he asked. He then kicked himself at her pained expression.

"No…I uh…"

"Tell you what, I'll go get the truck. Wave your arms when you see me so I can find you in the dark."

"Do I have to worry about any more of them coming out? I mean, aren't they supposed to be mean?"

"If you'd feel better, you can get the truck?"

"Uh…you do it. I just wish I would have brought a flashlight."

"Naw, don't feel bad. You brought me a sandwich."

THE WORLD BURNS

"That wasn't actually for you."

"I know." He laughed at her shocked expression and smiled. He leaned in and gave her a quick kiss on the lips and left before she found her voice again.

"What was that?" she called after him as he jogged away into the dark gloom. He could hear the smile in her voice.

§ § §

Blake butchered the hog when they got it in the barn and hung large cuts of it from the rafters. It was cooler in the barn than the outside, but he wasn't going to leave it for more than half a day.

"I've had a project I was always meaning to do."

"Oh yeah? What's that?"

"I was going to make my own smoker and then blog pictures of it and make an eBook out of it. I just never had the time."

"Do you need a hand now?"

"Sure. Let's get that dolly and go into the scrap pile."

In most old homesteads, folks never threw anything away, instead saving up broken appliances, jars, cans, etc., until they had enough to run it to the scrap yard or the dump. Blake's grandparents had done much of the same, and when his grandpa retired, he decided to fix appliances. In various states of use, there were probably twenty or thirty different appliances stored in the barn. One of them was an old upright freezer with wire racks.

"This is the one," he said, pushing the cart under it and moving it into the open doorway.

"What is that?"

"My smoke chamber. Come on, I'll show you."

They cut two circular holes into the freezer. One was down along the bottom and about six inches in diameter, and the other was a small one-inch diameter hole in the very top back corner. Blake kicked through his old pile of piping and came back with two pieces of black pipe about four feet long each. They had been from the old wood stove that his grandpa had used to heat that part of the barn. The first one fit perfectly into the bottom side of the freezer, and he left it hanging out a couple feet. He split the next pipe almost a third shorter and squeezed it into a somewhat circular shape. He pushed it in to test it for size, then pulled it out and made it about eight inches long with a hacksaw. He fit it in again and smiled.

"That's the hardest part."

"So where's the rest of it?"

"Come on, let's find something."

They went back into the pile and found a rusty cook stove. They brought it to the old freezer and set it down. Blake was thinking hard when apparently a light bulb went off in Sandra's head. She laughed and said, "I know, we can set the freezer on the old work bench and use an elbow to make the connection to the stove."

"That'll work. We'll have to play with the flue adjustments. We don't want to cook the food so

THE WORLD BURNS

much as smoke it."

"It's better than smoking it over an open fire."

"True," he smiled.

It took them another hour to get things set up the way that she'd envisioned. He'd need a ladder to get to the upper rack of the new "smoker," but it should work, in theory. The last thing he did, which he kicked himself for almost forgetting about, was put some wire screen mesh over the top hole. He held it in place by wrapping the pipe with bailing wire.

"To keep the critters out?"

"As much that as to keep a spark from coming out of the freezer and landing on something in here."

"Ready to fire it up?"

"I am."

They left one of the hams whole, but sliced everything else into strips that were an inch thick or less before filling the smoke chamber and firing it up for the first time. It was apparent that there was too much heat coming through the smoker chamber, so Blake brought the hacksaw out, and Sandra made some cuts to the pipe, making a small flap on the side. Her thoughts were that the smoke would rise higher than the heat, and the cut would let some of the heat vent out. They tested it, and that did the trick, so they wrapped the flap with more screen door mesh and bailing wire.

They kept the fire smoldering with downed fruit tree branches—pear wood and apple wood that was trimmed back every year from his small orchard. They had one more day before they would test the meat, so they made sure the fire was stoked before heading in to shower and go to bed. It had been a long week.

CHAPTER 7

Both of them awoke before the sun and hurried to get out the door first. Bacon had become the new obsession, and both were hungry to try it. Sandra squeezed out the door first, but stopped dead when she heard a buzzing sound. Blake crashed into her in his excitement and noticed her worried look right off.

"Somebody is coming."

"Why do you say that?"

"Listen," she told him, and he did. It almost sounded like the buzz of a chainsaw, but far off. It took him a moment to realize that he was hearing quad motors. More than one or two.

"Do you think one of them could be your dad, coming up here for you?"

"Dad doesn't have a quad."

"He could have found one."

Blake stepped inside. He grabbed his rifle and stepped back outside.

"You set up off the porch, Blake, to the side by the rain barrel."

"What are you going to do?"

"Stand here on the porch and see if they are friendly or not."

"What if they are not?" he asked, worried now.

"We'll convince them to leave." She pulled out her Beretta and held it in her right hand loosely by her side. "But if I tell you to shoot, don't let up until I call for you to stop."

Blake nodded and got into position. He knelt down and made sure his rifle was topped off and on safe. He could see the field in front of him through the gap between the barrel and the house, but to anybody coming up the hill, they'd have to be right on top of him to see him. He had no way to pre-aim the rifle without standing, so he just sat there on his haunches, waiting. Sandra gave him a quick smile and stepped down on the bottom step as three quads came racing up, the riders whooping and hollering to each other. Each of them had a pistol in hand, and one had a rifle strapped across his back.

Sandra held her hand up so they could all get a glimpse of her gun, and she trained it on them until they stopped over a hundred feet away.

"What do you want?" she called out, her voice harsh.

"We smelled the cooking. Figured we'd come

THE WORLD BURNS

up and see what's shakin', bacon," the middle rider said. He started laughing at his own joke.

"We don't have enough to share here. You guys go on back down the hill."

"Now lady, you aren't being very nice. Why aren't you being nice? Nervous without your husband here, perhaps?" the one on the left asked. Blake could just make out the tattoo on his face. Two teardrops. If it hadn't been done oversized and if the man hadn't turned just right, Blake would have missed it.

"Sorry guys, keep moving. Nothing here for you." She swung her gun up, pointing it in their direction. They all stepped off their quads.

"I take my turn first this time," the one on the right said, raising his gun and rubbing his crotch.

Blake took his first shot just as Sandra shouted. The biker on the right was blown off his feet by the crossfire, and the other two almost fell backwards in shock. The middle rider slid behind the quad and lifted his head up enough to try to take aim at Sandra. Blake had a funny angle, but took the shot anyways. His .30-06 blasted a hole through the flimsy plastic and fiberglass of the quad's body panel and knocked the man over on his back like he was a kicked mule. Blake worked the bolt on the gun as the last guy took off running for the woods that Holloway Lane was known for.

He centered the crosshairs of the scope on his back and was pulling in the slack from the trigger to take the shot when a distant shot rang out and the man tumbled.

"Oh shit, there are more of them?" he asked Sandra, half panicked.

"I don't know. That shot came from a ways off. Let's reload and get behind some cover."

She hurried off the porch and squeezed in behind the barrel, which was full from the last rain. It wouldn't stop every bullet, but it would stop quite a few. They waited until the sweat was trickling down the insides of their shirts and the bugs came out. A portly figure slowly walked out into the open, holding a rifle over his head.

"Who is that?" Blake asked.

"Let me see your gun," she replied.

He handed Sandra the rifle, and she held it up. She looked at Blake, smiled, and looked through the scope again before letting out a whoop of joy and taking off running. Blake could only check her progress with the scope and cover her as she ran towards the man.

"Daddy…" The words floated up to the pastor, and he smiled as his daughter jumped into his arms, knocking him over with the full-body hug. Blake smiled and lowered the rifle.

He checked to make sure the dead were really dead and tried not to look at the pair as they walked up the hill, their chatter running a mile a minute in excited voices. He stripped the raiders of guns and ammo and turned their pockets out, not finding much. He opened the pack strapped on the quad and stopped dead, his hand afraid to reach in when he saw what was inside.

"Hey Blake, it's my…" She rushed to his side, seeing him transfixed. "Don't touch those."

"I won't," he mumbled.

"What's got you two so spooked?" Pastor Duncan said, walking up and holding his hand out.

Blake shook it absentmindedly and nodded to the bag. The pastor looked inside and rubbed his chin a minute.

"If the pins had been pulled, they would have already gone off."

Inside were half a dozen grenades sitting on top of a package wrapped in plastic.

"Who are those guys?" he asked Blake and Sandra, who'd wrapped her arms around him in a tight embrace again.

"I think they are convicts."

"Why do you say that, Blake?"

"The tattoos on them. They look like gang tats."

"He's right, Dad. Look at this guy."

They poked around for a little bit, and then Blake loaded up the truck and drove the bodies out past the silo and dumped them into a shallow ditch. None of them wanted to spend the time and the effort to bury them, and it'd been obvious to all what their intentions were. Once Blake made it back to the house, he sat down at the tiny table in the kitchen to smell the agonizingly delicious aroma the frying bacon was making. Pastor Duncan had sliced it in thick slabs and was working the griddle while Sandra had her hands wrapped around a mug of coffee. Blake got some for himself and sat back and listened to Duncan tell his tale.

"…and when all the cars on the highway stalled out, I knew it was something bad. My watch and phone were dead, so I figured an EMP. I grabbed my bag and the case I keep my rifle in and walked towards Greenville. I saw the planes fly over me, and I turned to watch as they crashed. There were two of them, and it looked like they fell close to town. I headed north and tried to stay by the roads as much as I could. I traveled by night mostly, because on the third day, people got desperate. There was no water, the stranded motorists were starting to fight and steal from each other, and then some of the hard cases showed up."

"Hard cases?" Blake asked.

"The prison in Greenville. They had to do something with the prisoners, and less and less guards were showing up for work. Probably taking care of their families. They just opened the doors and ran before they could be caught. Rapists and murderers, along with the gentler purse snatchers, were suddenly free in a world without anyone to stop them. That's when I went into the woods and tried to avoid everyone."

"Oh my God, Daddy, was it bad out there?"

"The little town I skirted between here and there was on fire. Not from the planes, but from the looting. People were going crazy. Have you two had anyone else give you problems before today?"

"No," Blake admitted.

THE WORLD BURNS

"Well, if you guys plan on running that smoker for any length of time, you may want to put out extra security. I smelled it from miles away. It's how I homed in on you. When I got close, I could hear the quads coming, and I ran the rest of the way up here."

Blake couldn't help but look at the portly man before laughing at the thought. Soon Sandra busted up as well.

"What's so funny you two?"

"How many miles did you run, Daddy?"

"Well, it felt like all the way but…Say, you aren't making fat jokes when I'm making you bacon and fried potatoes, are you?"

"No sir," Blake came to a sobering end of the laugh. "About that security, what would we need? To fortify or whatever we need to do here?"

"Make it damn hard for anybody to even get up the lane. You're the only house up here, aren't you?"

"Yeah, my grandparents left me ten acres, but the rest of it is owned by a lumber company. They logged it years back and let my family farm it for something like a dollar an acre."

"Good. So nobody has any business back here?"

"What are you getting at?"

Pastor Duncan laid out his plan. It was devious, and his experiences in brush wars across the world became evident. He hadn't always been a holy man, only becoming a man of the cloth once his wife had died when Sandra was born. Still, it was scary how much about war and death the pastor knew.

CHAPTER 8

The next morning, Pastor Duncan got up early, having already given the two kids instructions on what they would need. He dressed in his camo outfit after letting it air out overnight and headed off down the lane. Today would be a day for making traps.

Blake and Sandra spent most of the previous afternoon scrounging in the barn for metal posts, old barbed wire, bailing wire, pipes, and scrap metal. The first thing they did was close in the lane where Blake drove along the fence line up to the house. Now it just looked like any other barbed wire cow pasture that was overgrown and ready for hay to be cut or cows to be let loose in it. They tried to brush out the tracks where the quads had come up as best as they could, and then they started with the tricks

THE WORLD BURNS

and traps.

Blake used a spool of monofilament fishing line. He and Sandra nailed old rat traps to trees about head high and loaded them. A small stick was jammed in the bottom of the tree to complete the lever, and they tied it off on the other side on small saplings. They brought out glow sticks from the camper and taped them in place. The theory was that you can't be everywhere at once unless you literally have an entrenched army close by, so an early warning system was what they were building. If somebody walked down the lane and stepped on or tripped on the monofilament line, it would pull the release on the rat trap, making it snap the glow stick. The illumination could be seen for quite a ways, and in the now quiet world, it would sound like the bark of a small rifle.

Another trap they made also utilized a rat trap. They drilled a hole and sanded through one end so a shotgun shell would rest inside of it. When the trap was sprung, it would hit the end of the shell. To set it off, they nailed a trim nail into the tree, leaving a small nub sticking out. The trap was nailed closed with the shotgun shell primer almost pressed tight against the nail. Dozens of these were set out, but they made Blake nervous. One wrong move and the shell would explode outwards instead of down a straight path to the barrel. The triggers were also set up using the monofilament. *Good thing grandpa hated rats*, Blake thought.

Then they pounded the sharpened pieces of

scrap at odd angles into the ground. Blake wrapped some rusty barbed wire around it tightly, making a tangle foot trap in random areas heading up to the house. They cut all the three-quarter-inch black and galvanized pipe they found in the barn down to about eight-inch lengths. Pastor Duncan then drilled screws into one-inch caps, the sharp point pointing into the pipe. The caps screwed onto six-inch pieces of one-inch pipe, and a shotgun shell was inserted into the three-quarter-inch pipe and then lowered carefully into the one-inch pipe.

The entire thing was buried to within an inch of the ground with the tops of the pipes wrapped in basic plastic wrap. The idea was to make what was called a toe popper, Pastor Duncan had explained. You step on the pipe sticking out, and the shotgun shell's primer goes off from the screw. Ugly, but effective. It wasn't hard to find enough materials to make two dozen.

Lastly, the junk in the barn was moved around to artfully hide the root cellar. A heavy slide lock was installed on the inside to use as a last resort panic room. They stored extra water and some of the pistols they got at the auction.

This work took most of the week, and Pastor Duncan spent most of his days watching from down the lane, trying to spot trouble before it came up. When Blake and Sandra weren't working at a feverish pace, they kept the garden watered and weed free and read more of the Foxfire books.

"It's too bad you don't have any livestock," Dun-

THE WORLD BURNS

can told him one night.

"Never needed any."

"It'd be nice to have eggs again."

"You know, I don't see any reason why we can't find some chickens someday. I don't have any feed for them, but they could forage and get scraps like my grandparents' chickens did."

"I wonder what it's like out there," Sandra pointed towards town.

"It's been a little more than two weeks since the grid went down. I got close to the end of the lane the other day using one of Blake's bicycles. There wasn't anybody around. I am curious though."

"Wait another week?" she asked her father.

"Yeah, probably. I don't know how bad it's going to be. The town could be gone, or the prisoners could have made it out here. Anarchy, Armageddon, you know…the end of the world as we know it." Duncan was deadpan when he said this, but was surprised by their reaction.

"*And I feel fine*," both Blake and Sandra sang out loud before their jaws dropped and they laughed. It was one of those surreal moments that ended with a big hug between the two while her father watched awkwardly.

"You know, since I've been here, I've stayed in the camper at night. It's got more than one bed."

"The bed in here is comfortable enough," Sandra said, and Blake turned four shades of crimson when he got the drift.

"No Sandra, he means…Pastor Duncan, Sandra and I tradeoff the bed for the recliner every other night. That way one of us can get some good rest and the other is close to the front door."

Relief washed through the old man's face and he fanned himself.

"Phew. I'd been meaning to ask, but in this day and age, I don't know if that's polite or…"

"Oh Daddy, stop. Both of you men look like you're going to have a heart attack."

Blake smiled at that and walked down to the basement. More to give them some time to talk, but he was also wanting to look at his store of food. A single person didn't touch his dried food stores as much as the three of them had, and more and more of his pest-proof buckets were emptying. The timing of the grid going down was horrible; he could have picked up the Azure Standard order from the farm and fleet store before his date with Sandra, but he had put it off, and he had to admit to himself, it was because he'd been distracted by her.

He'd thought about her plenty of times, and had grown comfortable and fond of her. Her energy and enthusiasm had made the hermit a little nervous more than once, but she'd grown on him. It was a struggle to keep his emotions in check now that her father was here. Love at first sight? Cupid had shot Blake true. He was smitten. He was pretty sure she felt the same way, but he worried that with the way things were, the timing was all wrong. He would wait.

Heavy footsteps came downstairs as he was

THE WORLD BURNS

running through Sandra's list of his dried goods, and a heavy hand touched his shoulder. Duncan was smiling when Blake turned to face him.

"I'm sorry about that. You two hit it off so well, and with you two being alone together...and me wanting to give you space, but I had this dad moment and—"

"Duncan," he said, using his name without pastor for the first time, "it's okay with me. Your daughter is very special to me, and I imagine to you. I just can't believe that I never ran into her before."

"Went to Catholic school." He smiled, and Blake laughed.

"Well you know what they say about...never mind," Blake cut off, turning a dark red.

"About the pastor's daughter, or Catholic schoolgirls or...?"

"I did it again. I'm sorry I didn't mean—"

Duncan laughed out loud and slapped a meaty hand against his shoulder and looked around the basement. "My daughter could do worse than you. You seem an honorable man. I'm sorry I doubted you."

"Well, we only had the one date."

"When we are safe, maybe you should make plans for a second one." Duncan winked and headed back upstairs.

"Wow."

CHAPTER 9

Everything had been quiet for another two weeks before they decided that with summer winding down, they should go get a better feel for what was happening in the world. They decided to use the quads from the convicts, knowing the speed and maneuverability would give them a better advantage, despite the sound they made. Duncan packed some tools in his kit, and they took off. Everyone had a rifle and gun on them, and they took a roundabout way to the end of the lane so they wouldn't have to reset any of their traps. Two gas cans were tied on to the back of Sandra's quad, which had the bigger storage area, and they headed into town.

Burned out buildings, cars with peeling paint from the intense heat, and all kinds of scrap and debris littered the town. Where the plane had crashed, the ground had been scraped clean, and the gas station in town was just a big hole in the ground with scorch marks. What didn't burn was flattened or simply blown apart by the explosive forces of the crashing plane. The wreckage was everywhere, as were the charred remains. The worst of it missed the church, and half of the Pastor's house was still standing.

They stopped and got off, killing the noisy gas engines so they could talk and check things out.

"Where is everybody?" Blake asked no one in particular. "There has to be survivors, somewhere."

"Probably in hiding, but I wouldn't count on finding survivors from around here," Sandra answered.

"How come?"

"The fire would have been too intense. People might be moving back into the area, like we are checking it out right now," Duncan said.

"Is there anything here you'd like to take back to the homestead?" Sandra asked, walking up to the exposed and charred skeleton of the house.

"No. It looks like it's a loss. I do have a cache of supplies on some state land that we might want someday. Mostly food."

"What about your guns, daddy?"

The pastor walked to the edge of the charred remains of his small house. "Gone. It was over there. Somewhere." He pointed vaguely.

The entire interior had burned, but somehow

two walls remained.

"We can pick through there and look," Sandra told him, putting her hand on her father's arm for comfort.

"There's no point. Let's—"

A shot rang out, and the three of them dropped down, Duncan slapping at his left shoulder. Crimson stained the material of his shirt and he grimaced in pain. Two more shots followed, hitting close to Sandra's prone form. She rolled behind the quad for better cover.

"Dad?" she shouted, worried.

"I'm okay. Hurts. Get eyes up there," he motioned with his head while pulling his pack off his shoulders, his eyes closing in pain.

"I can see them, two shooters. Both ducked down behind a burned out car," Sandra said, aiming her long gun scavenged from the convicts.

"If you get a shot…"

They all rolled tighter behind cover as more shots came in, this time from a new direction.

"Where are they?"

Duncan's rifle went off, and he watched for a moment before turning to Sandra and Blake.

"Somebody trying to be cute. Watch your sides."

Sandra's rifle barked three times as she took a shot, and two figures stood and bolted, trying to put distance between them. Her first shot toppled the figure on the left and missed the one on the right. The bolt action let out an empty click as she tried to fire a round that wasn't there. The angle was wrong for Duncan, but Blake dropped him with a snapshot before he could disappear between some wreckage.

"That was impressive," a wide-eyed Sandra whispered to Blake.

"I don't usually eat store-bought meat. Have to be a good shot, or I'd have to triple my garden."

"Is that all of them?" Duncan asked.

"I think so. Is it safe to come to you?"

"Blake? Come here, grab my pack from the quad," Duncan said. Blake could see he was sweating.

"I got it, Dad," Sandra interjected.

"No, you watch for more. Remember your training."

"Sorry Dad, I—"

"It's okay, sweetie," he told her calmly as she started to scan the distance for more shooters.

Blake made his way to Duncan in a crouching lope and pulled the pack down. He helped the pastor to pull his shirt off. Duncan's shoulder was bleeding profusely, the bullet having gone through the meaty part without hitting bone. They put a compress of gauze bandages on it, and used what looked like an ace bandage to hold the wads in place. Very carefully, Blake cut the sleeve off the shirt and helped the pastor put it back on.

"I don't see anything else," Sandra said after a pause.

"Okay girl, go check on them and make sure they are down. Grab the guns, ammo, and anything

BOYD CRAVEN

of use. I'm going to have Blake help me up, and we'll cover you from here."

Sandra took off, her gun following her line of site as she worked her way carefully to the first downed man who'd tried to shoot them on the side angle. Blake covered her while Duncan propped his rifle across the luggage rack of the quad and scoped the other areas. Sandra brought the supplies the man had to the guys and picked her way towards the man who had shot her father and his part-ner that almost got away. She found his backpack right off and emptied his pockets into it, then she headed towards where the last man fell. When she got there, she looked around and then looked back to Blake and Duncan. She pointed to the ground, questioning.

Duncan understood what she was asking right away and nodded yes. She looked down again and brought her rifle up, covering everywhere. Her ac-tions made Blake wary, and she soon turned, hiking back to them.

"What happened?" Blake asked her.

"The last man was gone."

"I must have just winged him."

"No, you got a solid spine shot on him," Duncan said, pain making rivulets of sweat drip off his face.

"So what does that mean?" Blake asked.

"That there's somebody else out here."

"We have to move."

"I know, I know. Let me think for a moment." He sat in silence for a little while, but Blake Inter-

70

THE WORLD BURNS

rupted.

"What if we head through the business district and avoid this section of town, then we can loop back through the park and head up to my place?"

"It's not a bad idea," Sandra added.

"Okay. Let's get this stuff strapped down and we'll split."

"Are you okay to drive?"

"I'll live. It hurts. It'll hurt worse when we get back and you have to open the wound up and clean it out."

"I don't know if I can do that, Dad."

"Don't worry Sandra, I can," Blake told her with a sad smile.

They had to make a few last-minute diversions—once when they saw someone darting from house to house, and again to avoid some wreckage. That had sent them down an industrial drive where they were weaving in and out of stalled cars and semis. The area seemed deserted, so they stopped and topped off the gas tanks from the jerrycans. Sandra took the chance to check on Duncan's bandages, and Blake wandered around the stalled trucks, thinking.

He opened the cab on a Wal-Mart truck and disappeared inside. When he got out, he was grinning ear to ear, carrying a clipboard. He handed it to Duncan to read and headed back to the rear door, smiling at the shiny new padlock holding the door closed.

"What's that?" Sandra asked the guys.

BOYD CRAVEN

"Well, it looks like your boyfriend here found us a big cache of stuff." He handed her the clipboard with the shipping manifest. Blake's face flushed, but Sandra was already reading the list and her eyes went wide as she read aloud.

"Dry goods, camping supplies, gardening…" She looked up. "This is the mother load, isn't it?"

"The lock is still intact in back. I don't have any tools with me to—"

"I brought some." Pastor Duncan rummaged with his good arm through the pack until he held up a crowbar.

Blake and Sandra tried two or three different ways to use it to break the lock open, but the opening of the hasp was either too small, or the end of the crowbar was too big. They considered beating it open, but worried that it would make too much noise, and they didn't want to attract attention to what they were up to. There had already been one gunfight and injury. In the end, they left it, but took the shipping manifest. The ride home left them on edge, but they made it there without any more troubles.

CHAPTER 10

A few days after Duncan's wound was cleaned out, it still didn't show signs of infection, so they all breathed a little bit easier. They kept the wound open so it could drain, and it was evident that although they had enough medical supplies to handle this one incident, more would be needed. Duncan spent his days watching the lane leading up to the homestead while Blake and Sandra kept the gardens weeded and watered. Produce was coming in heavy enough now that canning things was going to start taking a priority. The problem was, they didn't have enough hands to do everything they needed and not enough hours in the day.

They discussed letting their traps and tripwires take care of their early warning system so Duncan could free himself up and help them with food acquisition and storage, but it was decided that they'd rather take the pickup and the trailer to town to unload what they could out of the Wal-Mart truck and any other truck they found out there stalled. It amazed them that they'd never thought of it, and apparently it hadn't occurred to the desperate souls who had come after them.

One morning, while Blake and Sandra were working nonstop on the gardens, Duncan heard something slowly making its way through the underbrush towards the lane, so he moved deeper into the shadows of the stump he was sitting next to. He'd modified his camo outfit to a homemade ghillie suit from burlap and interwoven leaves and small twigs, so he looked like a stump himself when he sat still. He kept his gun low and waited. Soon he heard another sound, another branch snapping and a hushed whisper.

He took the safety off his gun. He saw the movement before he could make out the outline. Somebody was creeping through the woods with a shotgun in hand. He drew his gun up and rested it on the stump so he didn't have to strain his bad arm and settled the crosshairs on the lead figure. He didn't want to take the shot without knowing who it was or why. For all intents and purposes, the stranger could just be out hunting game. Then the man turned his head over his shoulder and whispered to someone behind him.

Duncan kept his gun on the first figure, but he

THE WORLD BURNS

let his eyes refocus and saw another dark shape. This one was moving more slowly, without as much grace. Soon he could see it was a figure dressed in dark pants and a dark hooded sweater or jacket. They were moving carefully, trying to choose every step to reduce the noise they made. The second person wasn't visibly armed, and was not having as easy a time as the one in front did stepping over taller branches or downed logs. One nasty stack had the figure stumble, and a third one that had been out of sight stepped forward to help the…woman?

Her hood had fallen aside, and she pushed her blonde-gray hair out of her eyes before the figure behind her held her arm and helped her to her feet and pointed silently.

"Thanks," she murmured so quietly that Duncan could barely hear it.

Trying to figure out if the woman was with the two men willingly or not would be the deciding factor in whether he would break cover or watch and wait. The woman rubbed the third figure's arm slightly, and they started off again. The leader finally made it to the edge of Holloway Lane and held up a fist. Their group stopped while he looked up and down the lane silently. He was close enough now that Duncan could see the camo face paint that had been obscuring his features. It was a young man, not much younger than his daughter. Things clicked into place for Duncan, and he decided to wait and see until the three of them walked up the lane.

"This is private property," Duncan boomed, training his gun on the surprised young man who dropped his own.

"Hey, wait!" the woman said, rushing to the young man's side. The last person in their group walked up, his rifle pointed to the ground.

The three of them looked around until a glint of sunlight reflecting off the scope had the woman pointing to the stump.

"Mister, please don't shoot us. We're just looking for a place to hide."

"Who are those young men?"

"My sons. We had to get out of town, you see—"

"Put the guns down, boys. I have you covered. Put them down and we can talk."

The boy's voices were angry, and he could only make out bits of the conversation. They wanted to fade into the woods, but their mother overrode them and shamed them into listening. They put the rifles down and undid their backpacks.

"Walk up the lane with your hands overhead."

They started up until Duncan could see no side arms were hidden in their waistbands. One of the boys had a knife, but out in the woods that was pretty standard equipment, and he probably didn't think it was anything special.

"That's close enough." He rose, throwing the hood of his ghillie mask back with one hand, holding his rifle on them with another. "Now, who are you, and why are you looking for someplace to hide?"

THE WORLD BURNS

"I'm Bobby Cayhill, that's my older brother Weston, and my momma is Lisa. We're being hunted by some convicts. About thirty of them."

"Thirty?"

"Yeah," Weston joined in. "They kicked in the door to my mom's house and were dragging her out when I jumped one of them. Bobby got the other. We didn't know there was going to be a ton of them. We were just trying to save her from…"

"Ma'am?" Duncan asked, not believing how fast things were falling apart in what remained of society.

"It's all true. I thought my boys were going to get killed but…they saved me from those animals. They were going to…One of them told me that they were going to take turns."

"How did the rest of them find out?"

"I tried to be quiet, but I got thrown off." Bobby looked sheepish. "So I grabbed my rifle and tried to make him go away. He just laughed at me, and I had to. There must have been a raid going down on our street. I didn't want to kill him and put us all in danger, I mean, I didn't have any other choice, did I?"

"No, no you didn't. Now, don't be alarmed, but I have to make a phone call and get the boss down here. You guys don't move. Got it?"

"Make a phone call? The EMP blew everything out."

"EMP? You know what, let's wait until the boss gets here. Everybody sit down Indian style for me please."

Duncan set his rifle on the stump and pulled his .357 and fired a shot. He waited five seconds and fired again. Waited five and fired one last time. The first shot made them jump, but his shot had been off to the side, in the ground. He reloaded quickly and waited. Within twenty minutes of silence, he could slowly hear twigs break and snap in the tree line behind the three family members. Weston tried to look over his shoulder, but Duncan warned him not to move. Just as had been planned, Blake and Sandra ghosted in behind them, their weapons drawn as they advanced slowly and stopped at the pile of weapons and gear, effectively putting the Cayhill's in a crossfire.

"Pastor Duncan?" Blake asked quietly.

"No, I'm Bobby, this is my brother—"

"He means me." He gestured with his bad arm for them to be quiet. "Found these three poking through the woods until they came across your driveway. Have the hogs been fed yet today?"

"No, they're still pretty hungry," Blake said, smiling and going along with the joke.

"Oh you two. Stop it, Daddy. You three, on your knees, cross one leg over the other and put your hands behind your head," Sandra commanded, moving quickly behind them, using the point of her rifle to poke them into moving faster.

She patted them down, tossing the knife behind her and apologizing to Lisa before frisking her thoroughly.

"Hey now," Bobby said. "Get your hands off—"

THE WORLD BURNS

"I'm just making sure." She backed off, leveling her rifle again.

"You guys can stand up and we can all talk now." She motioned for her Duncan and Blake to bring it in closer.

"We don't have much time," Lisa told them. "They said they were going to get the dogs."

"It's true. We lost them by walking upstream on the river, but I've heard them baying off and on for the last hour or so," Weston told them.

"Our dear lord in Heaven," Duncan intoned, crossing himself.

"Ma'am, I'd appreciate it if you lowered your rifle," Bobby walked toward her, hand out.

She stared at his hand a moment and handed the rifle to Blake, who was shooting the kid daggers with his eyes. She took the hand and executed a short but efficient hip toss and had him on the ground, his own arm pulled around his neck in a choke hold. The young man gasped in pain, and she quickly let go.

"Just remember to keep your hands to yourself, and I'm sure she won't hurt you," Blake told the shocked Bobby. Blake smiled as she hugged him and got her rifle back.

Bobby was smiling and rubbing his shoulder. "Sorry about that. End of the world and all…and you run into a pretty woman in the woods. Every guy's dream."

"But this girl is taken." Blake told him.

"I can see that. You'll have no problems from

me."

"Bobby, put it back in your pants, man. You're going to get us all killed." Weston told his younger brother.

"Boys will be boys. I'm Pastor Duncan, this short-haired Valkyrie is my daughter Sandra, and this is her boyfriend, Blake. It's his property we're on right now."

"So, tell us again what is going on, and who is coming?" Blake interjected.

Lisa began to talk, and everyone quieted down.

"I just wanted to wash the sheets. It happened because I wanted the bed not to smell like smoke and sweat. I'd hand-washed the sheets in a plastic tub with some Fels Naphtha soap and hung them out to dry on the clothes line out back. For the most part, we'd been staying indoors during the day, especially when people were acting poorly. Most of them left weeks ago. So I thought it was safe to hang out the sheets.

"I'd gotten everything pinned up just as Bobby had come back from carrying a bucket of fresh water from the river. I think Weston was upstairs when I heard the knock. I looked outside and saw three men. One of them was already looking through the window smiling. When they saw me, they kicked the door open. I screamed and ran. They caught me, but didn't know or care who else was around. They were filth; they promised rape and torture. My boys killed them, killed all of them. I wish they didn't have to, but they did, and now we have no-

THE WORLD BURNS

where to go and we're being hunted."

She broke then, and her quiet sobs filled the silence as her sons looked on, embarrassed.

"You boys did what you had to. Even God understands war, and protecting yourself and family," Duncan said softly, holding out a hand to them.

They all shook, and for once, Blake and Sandra lowered their rifles. They retrieved the guns and gear the travelers had been forced to drop, handing it back to them.

"We have to plan on repelling the invaders," Sandra said.

"They're not invaders, they're the scum that were let out of Greenville," Weston said.

"You've got decent guns. How good of a shot are you guys?"

"I'm okay. Weston is better."

"How good?"

"I always get a deer. Hit a lot more than I miss."

"Okay, I've got a plan," Sandra announced, her voice firm. "And Daddy, if you can think of something better, say it, otherwise we don't have time."

"Who is this woman?" Weston asked Blake.

"G.I. Jane," Blake answered.

CHAPTER 11

They led the Cayhills straight through the traps, leaving their scent behind as a trail. Duncan and Blake were very careful to point out every trap to them so as not to set them off. Carefully they walked through the tangle foot, and then through the toe tappers that were like a mine field. Sandra's plan had been simple and elegant and utterly ruthless.

A scent trail would be led towards the barn, and then they would double back, leaving Bobby to protect Lisa in the root cellar. The rest of them would take up position on the opposite side of the field that overlooked the lane. The thought was, the criminals would stay on the lane for easier travel until they started to run into the traps. They would lose some in the traps and then go into the field,

THE WORLD BURNS

straight into the shotgun rat traps and tangle foot. If they made it past that, the four of them would open up from behind cover and pray the toe tappers and their rifles would stop them from getting close to the house.

They all spread out behind cover, no one more than twenty feet away from each other, and waited. Duncan and Sandra prayed silently, and Blake kept a wary eye on Weston, still not sure about the younger man. They all seemed on the up and up, but Blake wasn't the trusting sort, not when their lives were on the line again and he'd just met the kid.

Everyone checked their weapons and hunkered down to wait. The day grew long, and the heat started to become unbearable. That was when they heard the first of the dogs. The dogs sounded close, and soon they heard the sounds of motors too. The vehicles stopped at the log that was rolled across the lane. A crackle of conversation was carried by the wind, and the dogs bayed again as a group emerged out of the woods to meet up with the groups in the pickup trucks, now barely visible in the fading afternoon light.

The dogs were pulling at the leashes, and the group seemed to come to a consensus, because they moved up the lane again. Someone made the decision to unleash the straining dogs, and they took off running. The bang of a shotgun shell trap rang out, followed by the pitiful cries of the dogs. There was cursing, and the sound somebody screaming.

BOYD CRAVEN

"Whoever shot my dogs, I'm going to kill you. You hear that? I'm coming for you."

The group surged, and more traps were set off. The glow stick traps were snapped, but they were not much help in the daylight. The shotgun shell traps went off as expected, and the group went chaotic and ran every which way, finding the barbed wire fence. They came to a full stop and huddled up to talk. They moved carefully as a group and stopped when they found a trap. They moved across them exaggeratedly. Taking their time.

"Why are they so bent on finding you guys?" Blake whispered over to Weston.

"One of the guys we killed was their leader's brother."

Blake nodded grimly, understanding now. He'd been having a hard time figuring out why the group just didn't turn back with the first traps. Was it pride? Was it anger? Were the Cayhills who they claimed to be? The little worry rat ran around his head, making him doubt everything. That's about when the convicts found the tangle foot trap, and the last man walking in line set off another shotgun-charged rat trap.

They surged away from the lane, which they'd found to be a deadly box of traps, and into the barbed wire. Five or six went down, tripping right away into the sharpened metal spikes the wire was wrapped around, hidden by the tall grass. The men who were impaled made horrible sounds. By Blake's count, there were still ten or twelve trying to pull their friends free, including a mountain of a man who was shouting orders. Duncan put his cross hairs on him and let out half a breath and pulled the trigger.

The burly man had luck; he was picking up a friend of his as the bullet left the barrel, exploding against the flesh of the man he was trying to help. The smaller man convulsed and died in the bigger man's arms, and the bigger man dropped him and hit the deck. With the quiet of the day broken by Duncan's gunfire, the four of them opened up on those they could see still standing. Two convicts crawled, and no one could get an angle on them as they ran up the hill. Blake unloaded his gun, trying to wing them, and he ducked down and reloaded while the remaining few of the raiders opened up on him, the tree he was hiding behind absorbing the lead.

"Sandra, I can't get a good angle on them, can—" He stopped; she wasn't there.

"Sandra?" Blake shouted. Duncan shook his head and motioned for him to look forward.

Peeking around the tree, he could see one or two of the convicts still trying to pull the living free from the barbed wire. Weston opened up on them with an SKS and both dropped. Blake put a bullet into a groaning man, and then everything was quiet. No one else was visible.

"Is that all of them?" Duncan asked Weston.

"No. Two of them got up the hill."

"Sandra is taking care of them. Blake, you go

make sure all of those guys are really dead. Be careful."

"You want me to do what?"

"Walk up, put a bullet in their heads."

§ § §

Weston and Duncan slowly went up the hill, working in cover until Duncan pointed out Sandra's still form lying prone with her rifle pointed to a clump of bushes. She looked back at them and gave them a sad smile and pointed at the clump with a free hand. Before anyone else could get their guns trained on them, two raiders broke cover and ran up hill, thinking they'd gotten out of the deadly box their friends had been in. They ran right into the toe poppers.

The shotgun shells went off as expected, and one man's leg completely disappeared as the heavy buckshot tore off everything from the knee down. The other tried to jump flat on the ground to hide from what he thought was more rifle fire, and he landed right onto another toe popper. The sound of it was muffled, a large hole blasting out the back of him, spraying the area with a red mist.

"Gross, but effective," Weston said, firing into the screaming man who was holding his stump, stilling his shrieks.

"Is that it?" Sandra asked.

"I think so, would you go help," he paused as Blake's .45 rang out, "Blake with mop-up and resetting the traps by the trail."

"Sure, what are you going to do?"

"I'm going to go check on Lisa and Bobby. We'll triple check everything, salvage what we can on these guys. Tell Blake to be careful on the lane, the traps may not have killed everyone and—"

"Daddy, I won't let anything happen to him. I really like him."

"I know you do, sweetie. Hurry then, and come back when you're done."

"Be safe, Daddy." She gave him a hug and worked her way carefully back to where the gunshots were coming from.

"Let's go get your brother and mom out of the cellar."

"Thank you. I mean it. Thank you."

§ § §

They approached the barn with caution, but everything was silent.

"Bobby, Lisa. Me and your boy are coming down, don't shoot," Duncan yelled.

Silence.

"You don't think…?"

Duncan could see the fear in the boy's eyes.

"Shhhh," he motioned. "Lisa, it's Duncan. Don't shoot."

They reached the bottom of the stairs and kept away from the doorway set into the stonework. Still silence. Duncan turned the knob and pushed the door open hard. He pulled his arm back as gunfire and sparks jumped off the stonework across from the door. Weston cried out as rock chips cut his face, and Duncan felt a warm trickle from his hairline. He used his sleeve to wipe at it and rolled into the room with his pistol ready. He came up behind the edge of one of the potato bins and got a glimpse of the massive convict that had dropped out of sight earlier. The man opened up with a semi-automatic pistol, his rounds causing mass murder in the spud world, but missing Duncan.

"Give me Weston. These three killed my brother. If you give me these three, I'll let you all go."

"I don't think you have room to negotiate here." Duncan peeked around the corner. The giant was covering the doorway, using Lisa as a human shield, her body pressed into his and one meaty arm around her neck. Tears streamed down her face, and smudges of dirt covered her clothes from what had to have been some sort of struggle.

Bobby lay on the floor limply, his shotgun lying on its side.

"Is Bobby okay?" Duncan yelled, seeing Weston in the doorway trying to look.

"I just gave him a good lump. If you have Weston come in here, I'll let you go. Hell, I'll give you the woman, how's that?"

"Why do you want them so bad?" Duncan pulled the .357 up and readied it for use.

"I told you. Give them to me, or I'll have this whole section burned to the ground. My men

THE WORLD BURNS

will—"

"Your men are dead," Weston said coldly, coming around the corner, his rifle raised.

Weston caught the giant by surprise. Both looked at each other, and the giant swung his gun hand around. Weston hesitated, not wanting to hit his mom by mistake, and the first bullet from the giant's gun spun him around and he fell to the ground over Lisa's screams. Duncan stood and fired. A small hole appeared in the center of the raider's head, and he fell backwards.

Coughing and holding his chest, Weston stood on wobbly feet, and for the first time, unbuttoned his camo gear. GPD was painted prominently across the vest he was wearing underneath, and he undid the Velcro and let it drop to the ground as Lisa rushed from first one son, then to the other.

"You okay, boy?" Duncan gave Weston a steadying hand.

"Yeah, hurts. Vest from work."

"Greenville Police Department?"

"Volunteer, second year." He coughed, massaging the spot over his heart.

"Help me with my mom and brother."

Bobby had a knot on his head, but came around quickly. With Lisa's help, he got them out of the cellar and up to the house where they sat on the porch, listening to the last of the gunshots.

"Don't go inside. There's more traps." Duncan pointed at the front door behind them. "Stay right here. I'm going to check on the kids."

89

CHAPTER 12

The trucks the raiders came in were unloaded and stashed in the woods, further back from the lane. The bodies had been dragged down into a low spot and left, and all the ill-gotten loot was carried into the barn to be sorted later. The Cayhills helped as much as they could, but Bobby was wobbly on his feet. Nighttime had them all in the empty house, and a few jokes were made about the "traps" that weren't there. Blake was silent as he considered what he was going to do next.

"Pastor Duncan, Sandra, can I talk to you a minute?" He motioned downstairs and they followed him.

"I know what you are going to ask, and yes, I think it's a good idea," Duncan told him.

THE WORLD BURNS

"Where would they stay?" Sandra asked.

"You know, I always planned on putting a room or two down here in the basement, I just never needed to. We could divide things up and…"

"That's if they want to stay," Duncan said quietly.

"Do you guys think it's a good idea?" Sandra asked him.

"We need more help. There just isn't enough of us."

"Do you think we can trust them?" Blake asked.

"They had their chance to kill us, plenty of times our backs were turned," Duncan said.

"Blake, sometimes you have to pray on it," Sandra said softly.

"Preacher's daughter." Blake laughed to himself under their baleful glares. "I was kidding."

And then they busted up laughing at his stricken expression.

"Now I know where she gets it from."

"Should we ask them tonight?" Sandra asked.

"I have one more thing I'd like to clear up before we ask them," Blake said.

"Oh, what's that?"

"I see how Bobby is looking at you, Sandra, and I know that you can take care of yourself, it's just that…"

"You scared that he'll steal me away?" She was smiling wickedly.

"No, it's just that…Sandra…Pastor Duncan. We've talked briefly, and I don't need a second date.

BOYD CRAVEN

Your daughter is everything that I ever wanted. With your permission, I'd like to…"

"Yes," he said, smiling.

"Sandra, will you be my wife?" He turned to her, all his love, fears, and insecurities showing in his eyes.

She jumped into his arms, kissing him deeply until her father tapped them on the shoulder, breaking the moment.

"Not married yet," he grumbled and walked upstairs.

Smiling, they both followed him a minute later.

"Was that a yes?"

"You couldn't tell?"

"My brain sort of exploded."

They walked out of the stairway hand in hand to see two shocked expressions on Weston's and Bobby's faces. Lisa and Duncan were locked in a kiss of their own.

"Uh…excuse me?" Sandra asked, confused and annoyed. "Not married yet," she scolded them.

"Besides, we have a lot to talk about, and even more to do," Blake said, closing the subject. "We have to make plans for the future."

—*THE END*—

To be notified of new releases, please sign up for my mailing list at: http://eepurl.com/bghQb1

ABOUT THE AUTHOR

Boyd Craven III was born and raised in Michigan, an avid outdoors-
man who's always loved to read and write from a young age. When
he isn't working outside on the farm, or chasing a household of kids,
he's sitting in his Lazy Boy, typing away.

Facebook: https://www.facebook.com/boyd3

Email: boyd3@live.com

You can find the rest of Boyd's books on Amazon.

13560158R00060

Printed in Poland
by Amazon Fulfillment
Poland Sp. z o.o., Wrocław